Katy Duck

Is a Caterpillar

By Alyssa Satin Capucilli Illustrated by Henry Cole

For Peter and Laura, who love to dance! —A. S. C.

For Caroline, my little butterfly —H. C.

LITTLE SIMON

An imprint of Simon & Schuster Children's Publishing Division

New York   London   Toronto   Sydney

1230 Avenue of the Americas, New York, New York 10020

Text copyright © 2009 by Alyssa Satin Capucilli • Illustrations copyright © 2009 by Henry Cole

Manufactured in the United States of America

First Edition

2 4 6 8 10 9 7 5 3 1

ISBN-13: 978-1-4169-6061-4   ISBN-10: 1-4169-6061-9

Katy Duck loved to dance.

Katy Duck loved to twirl like a snowflake on a frosty winter day.

She loved to sparkle like a star on a warm summer's eve.

And in the fall Katy loved
to spin like a leaf, softly
tumbling to the ground.

"Tra-la-la! Quack, quack!
How I love to dance!"
said Katy Duck.

Spring was Katy's favorite season of all. Springtime was filled with new and exciting surprises. Why, in springtime amazing things happened right before your eyes.

Katy stretched like the buds that magically blossomed on the trees. Katy hopped to and fro, like the baby birds just learning to fly. Katy swayed in the breeze like the tulips poking their heads above ground.

"Tra-la-la! Quack, quack! How I love to dance!" said Katy Duck. "Tra-la-la! Quack, quack! How I love spring!"

"Come along now, Katy Duck," said Mrs. Duck. "You don't want to be late for dance class."

When Katy arrived at Mr. Tutu's School of Dance, the other dancers were abuzz with excitement.

"Our dance recital is in just a few weeks. It will be a special celebration of spring," said Mr. Tutu. "There will be flowers swaying in the breeze. There will be swans floating on the lake. There will be birds hopping to and fro. Now, practice, everyone. Practice! In a few moments I will announce your part in the show."

A show to celebrate spring! Katy Duck couldn't be more excited. She could hardly wait to see which part Mr. Tutu would select for her.

Katy imagined that she was a bright yellow daffodil. She stretched up on her tiptoes. She could feel the spring breeze rustling through her petals. She could wear a sparkly costume, too.

"Why, that's one of the most beautiful spring flowers I've ever seen!" said Mr. Tutu.

Next, Katy imagined she was a swan on the lake. She glided. She floated. She could just imagine a beautiful costume with shimmering wings!

"Yes, yes," said Mr. Tutu. "That's a wonderful swan, Katy Duck."

And then Katy waved her arms up and down, up and down. She flitted here. She flew there. She curled to the ground as if she was landing in a soft, cozy nest.

"I'm certain that's one of the best birds ever," said Mr. Tutu. "Well done, Katy. Well done."

Before long it was time to announce who would be assigned each part.

"Gather around, please," said Mr. Tutu. He rubbed his chin. He cleared his throat. Katy's heart beat with excitement. Which part would be hers?

First, Mr. Tutu chose the spring flowers. But he did not choose Katy Duck.

"That's okay," said Katy. She did want to be a pretty flower, but she could be a beautiful swan, or a fuzzy baby bird, or even a colorful ladybug. Katy Duck stretched her neck gracefully and waited.

Next, Mr. Tutu chose the spring swans. But he did not choose Katy.

"Oh, my," said Katy, thinking of the shimmering wings. "I would love to be a swan."

Mr. Tutu chose the birds. There were baby birds just learning to fly! But he did not choose Katy.

Oh, no, thought Katy. She really, really wanted to be a bird.

Then Mr. Tutu chose blossoms, trees, a sun, and some fluffy clouds. "I believe we have everything we need for a wonderful celebration of spring," said Mr. Tutu.

"But what about me?" asked Katy Duck.

Mr. Tutu turned to Katy. He rubbed his chin. He cleared his throat. He looked at Katy thoughtfully.

"Oh yes, of course," said Mr. Tutu. "You, Katy Duck, shall be a caterpillar."

A *caterpillar?* thought Katy Duck. A caterpillar crawled on the ground. A caterpillar did not sway or glide or flutter. A caterpillar did not have petals or sparkles. Katy felt a lump in her throat. Her stomach ached. Katy tried very hard not to cry.

"Imagine, Katy Duck," said Mr. Tutu, "a caterpillar. What would a celebration of spring be without a caterpillar?"

Katy looked right. Katy looked left. Katy looked down.

This was not the part Katy had hoped for at all.

The class practiced and practiced and practiced.
They practiced and practiced some more.

While the flowers swayed, Katy Duck stretched.

While the swans floated, Katy inched up and down.

While the birds flew to and fro, Katy jiggled and wiggled.

At last it was time for the show.

"Places, everyone. Please take your places!" called Mr. Tutu.

The curtain swept open. The music began. The flowers burst forth onto the stage. The swans glided along oh-so-gracefully. The baby birds flapped their wings, skittering to and fro. Buds blossomed and trees swayed. Clouds skipped by. The sun shone its rays.

The audience applauded. It was a wonderful celebration of spring, indeed.

Now it was time for Katy Duck's entrance. Mr. Tutu nodded.

"Imagine, Katy Duck," said Mr. Tutu, "a caterpillar."

Katy Duck slowly crawled like a caterpillar onto the stage.

She inched up and down.
She stretched.
She curved. She jiggled.

She wiggled. She inched up and down some more.

And then something happened. Suddenly Katy Duck remembered just why spring was her favorite season of all. Springtime was filled with new and exciting surprises. Why, in springtime amazing things happened right before your eyes.

Katy spun around quickly. Katy curled up. Then Katy lay absolutely still.

The audience grew quiet. Very quiet.

And when it was just the right time, Katy jiggled and wiggled again. Katy rocked and rolled. She bounced and she bumped. Katy reached, and Katy stretched. As the music soared, Katy Duck felt her arms begin to flutter. She felt her feet begin to pitter-patter.

And there, right before everyone's eyes, came a true springtime surprise, something new and exciting and amazing, indeed. Why, even Mr. Tutu had never seen anything quite like this before.

Where there once was a caterpillar, there now appeared a butterfly! And after all, what would a celebration of spring be without a butterfly?

Katy Duck fluttered and floated and flew proudly across the stage.

"Bravo!" cried the crowd as the flowers bowed. "Bravo!" they cheered as the swans curtsied. "Bravo!" they applauded as the baby birds flapped their wings.

But the biggest cheers of all were saved for Katy Duck.

"Bravo, Katy!" cried Mr. Tutu.

"Tra-la-la. Quack, quack! How I love to dance!" said Katy. "Tra-la-la. Quack, quack! And how I do love spring!"